Ruby's School Walk

For Emily — for making sure I kept Ruby on the path — K. W.
To Pete, Sarah and Rob for your invaluable contribution xx — M. L.

Barefoot Books
294 Banbury Road
Oxford, OX2 7ED

Text copyright © 2010 by Kathryn White
Illustrations copyright © 2010 by Miriam Latimer
The moral rights of Kathryn White and Miriam Latimer have been asserted

First published in Great Britain by Barefoot Books, Ltd in 2010
This paperback edition first published in 2012

Graphic design by Barefoot Books
Reproduction by B & P International, Hong Kong
Printed in China on 100% acid-free paper
This book was typeset in Triplex and Hoagie Infant
The illustrations were prepared in acrylic paints
and watercolour pencils

ISBN 978-1-84686-785-9

British Cataloguing-in-Publication Data:
a catalogue record for this book is available from the British Library

1 3 5 7 9 8 6 4 2

Ruby's School Walk

Written by **Kathryn White**
Illustrated by **Miriam Latimer**

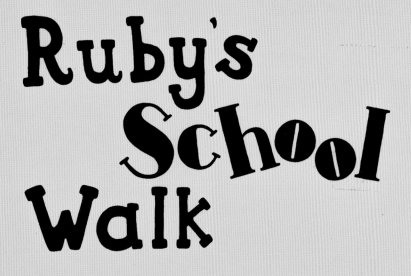

Barefoot Books
Step inside a story

On the way to school
there's a rushing river.
It's full of **crocodiles**.

Mum says, 'It's just the stream,
with silver fish and frogs and logs.'
But she's wrong.
I must be brave, I must be strong.

Those crocodiles may
be out of sight, but
they're ready to
snap, **roar** and **bite**.

I've seen their long tails
swirling round

Between the reeds,
without a sound.

So I dance on the bank
in the morning sun,

And my **giant** shadow
makes them run.

On my way to school there's a **haunted** house.
It's full of ghosts.

Mum smiles. She says,
'It's just an empty place for sale.'
But she's wrong.
I must be brave, I must be strong.

I've seen dark shadows float about,
And **bats** with red eyes peering out,
And **witches** flit around the rooms,
And outside, I've seen witches' brooms.

So I sing my special magic song,
And do my magic **hopalong**.

On my way to school there's a **tiger** hiding behind a wall, Mum smiles.

She says, 'That's just
Old Fletcher's tabby cat.'
But she's wrong.
I must be brave, I must be strong.

I've seen it open up its jaws
And bare its fangs and jagged claws.
I've seen it **crouch**

                    and **sneak**

                              and **prowl**.

So I bark my loudest, like a hound,
And **growl** and leap and jump

                              and **bound**.

On my way to school
There's a forest
deep and **dark**.

Mum smiles. She says,
'It's just the trees in the park.'

But she's wrong.
I must be brave, I must be strong.

The forest's full of **mighty beasts**.
They're hunting round for tasty feasts.
They **loom**, they **lurk** behind the trees,
And call each other on the breeze.

So I shout, 'Look out, beasts!
Keep well back!
I've brought my sword,
So don't attack.'

At my school, I'm not so sure.

Mum walks with me through the door.

My heart beats fast, my feet go slow.

Mum hangs my bag and turns to go.

I wonder what I'll do today.
I don't know what to think or say.

Mum smiles. She says,
'Ruby, perhaps today you will be
Finding **treasure** in the sea;

Catching **dragons** in the sky,
And teaching **fairies** how to fly;

You'll be teaching
trolls to read and write,
and painting **stars**
to make them bright;

You'll be sailing **ships** across the sea,

and setting helpless **mermaids** free.'

I hug her so;
I know she's right.

I say, 'Bye, Mum,
See you tonight!'